CU00798587

D E F I N I T I V E   E D I T I O N S

BAD SCIENCE

JUDGE DREDD

GUNGE

by *John Wagner, Alan Grant* and *Ron Smith*

ZOMBIES

by *John Wagner, Alan Grant* and *Cliff Robinson*

THE BLOOD OF SATANUS

by *Pat Mills* and *Ron Smith*

MONKEY BUSINESS AT THE CHARLES DARWIN BLOCK

by *John Wagner, Alan Grant* and *Mike McMahon*

THE WEATHER MAN

by *John Wagner, Alan Grant* and *Ron Smith*

THE AGGRODOME

by *Kelvin Gosnell* and *Mike McMahon*

MANAGING DIRECTOR
PETER BARBER

PUBLISHING DIRECTOR
JON DAVIDGE

U.S. SALES DIRECTORS
SAL QUARTUCCIO
BOB KEENAN

MANAGING EDITOR
STEVE MacMANUS

GRAPHIC NOVEL EDITOR
STEVE EDGELL

DESIGN
RIAN HUGHES for the SCIENCE SERVICE

Cover painting by *Brendan McCarthy*

Interior coloring created by *Damon Willis*

Definitive Editions produced by *Bob Keenan* and *Sal Quartuccio*

Published by Fleetway Publications, Greater London House, Hampstead Road, London NW1 7QQ, a member of Maxwell Consumer Publishing & Communication Ltd. Distributed in the UK by Amalgamated Book Services, 408 Vale Road, Tonbridge, Kent, TN9 1SW and IPC Marketforce, Kings Reach Tower, London SE1 9LS. US Representation and Marketing: SQP Inc, PO Box 4569, Toms River, New Jersey 08754, USA. Sole US Distributor: Titan Distributers, 206 41st Street, Brooklyn, NY 11232, USA. No similarity between any of the names, characters, persons, and/or institutions in this book with those of any living or dead person is intended, and any such similarity which may exist is purely coincidental. Printed in Spain by Cronion SA, Barcelona. Copyright © 1990 Fleetway Publications. All rights reserved. First edition December 1990. ISBN 1 85386 230 4

3

4

HERE— HAVE A *CHOC-O-HAIR* BAR! REAL TASTY!

THANKS. I'LL GIVE IT A MISS.

IT'S ALL STRICTLY LEGAL, JUDGE DREDD! THERE'S NO LAW AGAINST EATIN' BUGS AN' THINGS!

MAYBE NOT. BUT I WANT SAMPLES OF EVERY GUNGE PRODUCT TO JUSTICE DEPARTMENT LABS FOR ANALYSIS BY NOON TODAY!

TEK-JUDGES SUBJECT THE GUNGE PRODUCTS TO A FULL BATTERY OF TESTS—

THE COOKING PROCESS REMOVES ALL HARMFUL ELEMENTS FROM THE INGREDIENTS. THEY'RE TOTALLY HYGIENIC, HIGHLY NUTRITIOUS—AND, IN SOME CASES, VERY, VERY TASTY!

HERE, CHIEF JUDGE— TRY A *KRISPY SLUG FLAKE.*

NO THANK YOU.

IT'S LEGAL, THEN? FAIR ENOUGH. IF THE CITIZENS WANT TO EAT IT, SO MUCH THE BETTER!

WITH JUSTICE DEPARTMENT'S SEAL OF APPROVAL BEHIND HIM, OTTO SUMP IMMEDIATELY LAUNCHES A RANGE OF *NEW GUNGE RECIPES*—

TAKE A TIP FROM *CAPTAIN GUNGE*— TRY MY NEW *CAPTAIN'S PIE*! IT'S FULL OF SEA-SLUGS, CRUSHED SHELLS, LIMPETS... NOT FORGETTING PLENTY OF OLD FASHIONED *SWAMPWEED*! ALL PRE-CHEWED, OF COURSE, AND TOPPED WITH A RICH SQUID-INK SAUCE!

A DRINK WITH YOUR MEAL, SIR? LET ME RECOMMEND *GUNGE "BLACK WIDOW" SPIDER WINE*, MATURED IN OLD BOOTS FOR MORE THAN A WEEK, AND BROUGHT TO YOU COURTESY OF *OTTO SUMP*!

MR GUNGE BAKES EXCEEDINGLY DISGUSTING CAKES!

BUT A STRONG BACKLASH OF OPINION IS GROWING, LED BY THE CITY'S *MORAL HEALTH COMMITTEE*—

SEE HERE, CHIEF JUDGE— WE WANT THESE *GUNGE* PRODUCTS *BANNED*! THEY'RE POSITIVELY *UNHEALTHY*!

ON THE CONTRARY! KILO FOR KILO, GUNGE IS *TWICE* AS NUTRITIOUS AS *PRIME MUNCE*!

B-BUT MAGGOTS AND MOULD AND SLIME AND SLUDGE — IT'S NOT RIGHT! IT'S DOWNRIGHT INDECENT!

NEVERTHELESS IT'S LEGAL, CITIZEN!

MY COMMITTEE WON'T STAND FOR IT! WE'RE GOING TO ORGANISE PUBLIC OPINION AGAINST THIS OTTO SUMP!

BE SURE YOU ORGANISE IT LEGALLY!

THE FIRST PROTESTS TAKE PLACE THAT DAY, WITH MASS SIT-INS OUTSIDE SUMP FAST-GUNGE OUTLETS—

♫ WE SHALL NOT BE MOO-O-OVED! ♫

GUNGE GORGERY

GUNGE DEPRAVES

BAN GUNGE

PROTEIN OR DIE

NO TO GUNGE

BAN GUNGE

RAPI-GUNGE

EAT AT GUNGE-U-LIKE

GUNGE SCREU!

BAN GUNGE

SAY NO TO GUNGE

ILLEGAL DEMO. OBSTRUCTION. SIX MONTHS! START CARTING 'EM AWAY!

BUT THE ARRESTS MERELY SERVE TO FAN THE GROWING ANTI-GUNGE FEELING—

THIS IS ISO-CUBE NINE-FOUR-FOUR! WE GOT A THREE-WEEK BACKLOG HERE! YOU EITHER GOT TO STOP ARRESTING THESE GUNGE PROTESTORS—OR START BUILDING SOME NEW ISO-CUBES!

6

FOR ONCE, PUBLIC OPINION HOLDS SWAY AT THE JUSTICE DEPARTMENT—

WHAT DO WE DO, DREDD? WE'VE GOT TO BAN GUNGE PRODUCTS TO END THIS MASS DISORDER – BUT WITH FOOD SHORTAGES THE WAY THEY ARE, WE CAN'T AFFORD TO LOSE SUCH A RICH SOURCE OF NUTRITION!

GUNGE PROTESTS ARREST LEVEL

THERE'S ONE THING WE CAN DO!

AND SOON...

OTTO SUMP, I HAVE A COMPULSORY PURCHASE ORDER ON YOUR ENTIRE GUNGE PRODUCTS INDUSTRY. I'M CLOSING YOU DOWN!

AW, JUDGE DREDD! NOT AGAIN! CAN'T WE TALK ABOUT THIS?

NO!

OVERNIGHT, OTTO SUMP'S GUNGE EMPIRE DISAPPEARS. THE PUBLIC MIND IS AT REST.

CLOSED
GONE AWAY

CLOSED OWING TO BANNING OF GUNGE

MEANWHILE, OTTO'S VAST STOCK OF GUNGE INGREDIENTS IS TAKEN TO A SECRET FACTORY SOMEWHERE IN THE CITY. THERE IT IS MASHED AND PULPED UNTIL IT IS TOTALLY UNRECOGNISABLE—

THE NEXT DAY, JUSTICE DEPARTMENT'S NEW RANGE OF FOODSTUFFS IS LAUNCHED —

FOODSTUFF A
FOODSTUFF B
FOODSTUFF C

BECAUSE THEY CARRY THE JUSTICE DEPARTMENT GUARANTEE, NO INGREDIENTS ARE LISTED.

WHAT THEY DON'T KNOW WON'T HARM THEM!

YES. SOMETIMES A LITTLE DECEPTION IS NECESSARY, FOR THE GOOD OF THE PEOPLE!

EPILOGUE: IN THE ISO-CUBE WHERE THE MORAL HEALTH COMMITTEE IS LANGUISHING —

SOME NEW GRUB FOR YOU, TODAY – THE GUARANTEED, JUSTICE DEPARTMENT-APPROVED FOOD!

MM-MMM! DELICIOUS! IT MAKES OUR PROTESTS ALL WORTHWHILE!

NEXT: ZOMBIES

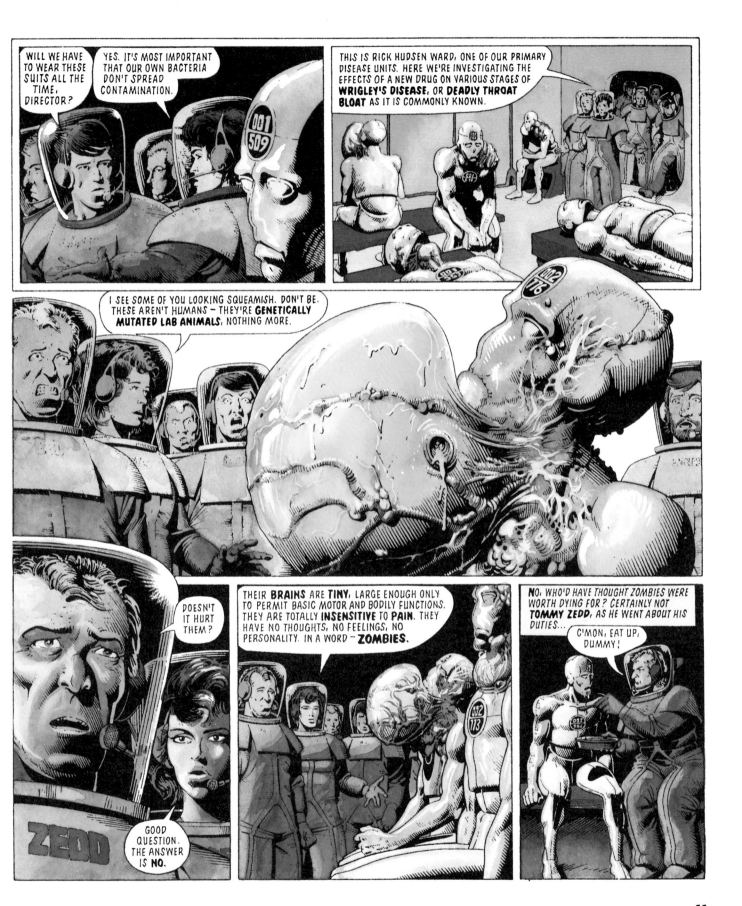

HE WAS DETERMINED TO MAKE A GO OF IT, KEEP HIS NOSE CLEAN...

THINK OF THEM LIKE SLABS OF MEAT, THAT WAS THE SECRET.

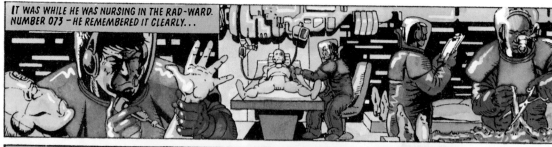

IT WAS WHILE HE WAS NURSING IN THE RAD-WARD. NUMBER 073 – HE REMEMBERED IT CLEARLY...

IN ITS DEATH THROES IT HAD TURNED ITS SIGHTLESS FACE TO HIM AND ITS HAND HAD STRETCHED OUT, GRIPPED HIS WRIST –

– AND SQUEEZED.

THIS ONE'S DEAD.

DID YOU SEE THAT – IT SQUEEZED MY HAND!

LIKE IT WAS TRYING TO TELL ME SOMETHING...!

DON'T BE ABSURD. JUST A MUSCLE SPASM.

BUT FROM THAT DAY, TRY AS HE MIGHT, TOMMY ZEDD COULD NO LONGER SEE HIS CHARGES AS MERE MEAT. THEY HAD BECOME... HUMAN.

EAT UP, STEVE. GOT TO KEEP YOU HEALTHY.

JUDGE DREDD

PROLOGUE: *SATANUS — THE BLACK TYRANNOSAUR — WAS REINCARNATED BY A MIRACLE OF MODERN SCIENCE...*

AND NOW, IN A *GENETIC RESEARCH LABORATORY* IN *MEGA-CITY ONE*... CITY OF THE FUTURE —

IN HERE, WE HAVE A *PLASMA-BASED SECRETION*, TAKEN FROM THE BODY OF SATANUS BEFORE HE ESCAPED INTO THE CURSED EARTH...*

...FROM IT, A *NEW TYRANNOSAUR* CAN BE GROWN!

SADLY, THE JUDGES HAVE *BANNED* SUCH EXPERIMENTS AS BEING TOO DANGEROUS.

* SEE THE CURSED EARTH PART TWO

CYRIL J. RATFINKLE WAS WELL KNOWN FOR ASKING STUPID QUESTIONS...

WHAT WOULD HAPPEN IF SOMEONE *DRANK* THAT LIQUID, SIR?

NOW GO AND PHOTOCOPY THESE NOTES, RATFINKLE.

IT'S ALL YOU'RE GOOD FOR!

IDIOT! WHO IN HIS RIGHT MIND WOULD DRINK *TYRANNOSAUR BLOOD?*

WHEN I JOINED THIS LAB, I'D THOUGHT I'D BECOME A GREAT SCIENTIST— NOT A *LACKEY!* BUT I'LL SHOW THEM THERE'S MORE TO CYRIL J. RATFINKLE THAN PHOTOCOPYING AND FILING!

I'LL SHOW THEM WHAT HAPPENS WHEN SOMEONE... *DRINKS THE BLOOD OF SATANUS!*

2000 A.D.
Credit Card:

SCRIPT ROBOT
PAT MILLS
ART ROBOT
RON SMITH
LETTERING ROBOT
TOM FRAME

COMPU-73E

OH, NO... THOSE *BONES!* MRS POTTS' ALIEN!

REX! WHY— WHY ARE YOU LOOKING AT ME LIKE THAT?

GET OUT, LYNSEY! JUST *GET OUT* — BEFORE IT'S TOO LATE!

REX — YOU'VE GOT TO SEE A DOCTOR!

FORGIVE ME, LYNSEY. I—I HAD TO SEND YOU AWAY. I DON'T UNDERSTAND IT — BUT SOMETHING *EVIL* IS *GROWING INSIDE ME!*

SHORTLY AFTER, JUDGE DREDD WAS BESIEGING A BUILDING, WHEN—

BANG! BANG!

SORRY TO INTERRUPT YOU, JUDGE DREDD, BUT I GOT A WOMAN HERE WON'T SPEAK TO ANYONE BUT YOU. LYNSEY PETERS. SOUNDED URGENT — I'M PATCHING HER IN.

LYNSEY EXPLAINED —

HE PILED UP THE FURNITURE — LIKE HE WAS BUILDING HIMSELF... *A NEST!* JUDGE, I NEED YOUR HELP!

LADY, YOUR HUSBAND HAS COMMITTED NO CRIME! RIGHT NOW I GOTTA DEAL WITH A CREEP WHO'S HOLDING A COUPLE OF KIDS HOSTAGE!

BUT THIS COULD BE SERIOUS, TOO!

IT'LL HAVE TO WAIT! I GOT A CRAZY PUNK HERE TO HANDLE... ...AND I'M GOING IN — *NOW!*

NO, JUDGE! THE MAN NEEDS HANDLING WITH KID GLOVES — HE'S EMOTIONALLY DISTURBED!

MY TEMPER AIN'T TOO GOOD, EITHER!

BANG!

SOMETHING HORRIBLE WAS HAPPENING TO LYNSEY PETERS' HUSBAND, REX. *BLACK SCALES* BEGAN APPEARING ON HIS BODY AND HE DEVELOPED A STRANGE TASTE FOR *RAW MEAT*. THEN, AS LYNSEY RETURNED HOME...

THAT—THAT THING—IT— IT CAN'T BE MY HUSBAND!

JUDGE DREDD
BLOOD OF SATANUS : PART 2.

REX—IT'S ME! NO—PLEASE!

AAAAH

THE CREATURE DRAGGED THE BODY OVER TO ITS NEST, AND BEGAN TO FEED...

2000 A.D.
Credit Card:
SCRIPT ROBOT
PAT MILLS
ART ROBOT
RON SMITH
LETTERING ROBOT
TOM FRAME
COMPU-73E

IN THE FLAT ABOVE, CYRIL J. RATFINKLE WATCHED THROUGH A HOLE IN THE FLOOR...

THE METAMORPHOSIS IS COMPLETE! I HAVE CREATED A NEW SPECIES — *HOMO-TYRANNOSAURUS!*

EARLIER, RATFINKLE HAD TRICKED REX INTO DRINKING THE BLOOD OF SATANUS.

THE CREATURE HAS DEVOURED ITS VICTIM AND IS NOW LEAVING ITS NEST — NO DOUBT TO FIND FURTHER PREY...

THIS WILL SHOW PEOPLE THERE'S MORE TO CYRIL J. RATFINKLE THAN TAKING PHOTOCOPIES!

QUESTION : WHEN THE VICTIM WAS ATTACKED, SHE APPEARED PARALYSED WITH TERROR...

...WHAT MAKES US HUMANS SO AFRAID OF BEING EATEN ALIVE ?

IS IT THE THOUGHT OF...

SHARP TEETH...

SINKING INTO SOFT FLESH ?

...OR IS IT THE FEEL OF HOT ANIMAL BREATH ON THE BACK OF YOUR NECK ?

OH MY GOD! IT — *IT'S HERE!*

SOME TIME LATER...

YES... THIS IS LYNSEY PETERS, JUDGE DREDD!

DROKK! SO HER CRAZY STORY WAS TRUE AFTER ALL!

ANOTHER INNOCENT CITIZEN DEAD — AND ALL BECAUSE OF *STUPIDITY!*

BUT, JUDGE DREDD — THERE WAS NOTHING WE COULD DO... NOTHING *SHE* COULD DO!

SHE COULD HAVE LEFT US HER ADDRESS!

THE REMAINS OF A NEIGHBOUR, *RATFINKLE*, WERE ALSO FOUND IN THE *"NEST"*. HE WORKED AT A GENETICS RESEARCH LABORATORY. THIS IS RATFINKLE'S BOSS.

WE'RE GOING TO MISS HIM. RATFINKLE WAS AN EXCELLENT PHOTOCOPIER... REALLY CRISP, CLEAR COPIES!

AFTER DREDD HAD QUESTIONED THE SCIENTIST...

ACCORDING TO RATFINKLE'S *TAPES*, THIS TYRANNOSAUR BLOOD HAS TURNED PETERS INTO A... *MAN-BEAST?*

BUT THE TYRANNOSAUR'S *LUST* FOR BLOOD MUST SOON BE *SATISFIED*, JUDGE. IT WILL NEED TO *EAT* AGAIN *SOON* — AND IN *GREAT QUANTITIES*.

AND IT'S OUT THERE SOMEWHERE — ON THE STREETS!

MEANWHILE, REX PETERS HAD BECOME HUMAN AGAIN...

I'M SO *ASHAMED*... HOW COULD I HAVE DONE SOMETHING SO *FOUL?*

AND WHEN WILL I DO IT AGAIN?

YES. THE METAMORPHOSIS WOULD BE *UNSTABLE* AS MAN AND BEAST *FIGHT* FOR *CONTROL* OF THE BODY!

SHORTLY AFTERWARDS —

WE GOT YOUR CALL, CITIZEN.

I'VE GOT *NOTHING* LEFT TO LIVE FOR! GOTTA *END* IT ALL... BEFORE — BEFORE THE *BLACK SCALES* COME BACK!

IT—IT'S MR PETERS, JUDGE! HE WANTED TO GO UP TO HIS OFFICE *AT THIS TIME OF NIGHT*...

JUDGE DREDD

A BEAST WITH THE CUNNING OF A **MAN** AND THE STRENGTH OF THE GREATEST **CARNIVORE** THAT EVER WALKED THE EARTH! THAT WAS **REX PETERS** – THE MAN WHO DRANK . . .

THE BLOOD OF SATANUS!

THE MAN WHO WAS NOW GOING TO EAT – *JUDGE DREDD!*

RIPPPP

UUUHH!!

TEARRRRR

GOTTA...GOTTA REACH MY *DAGGER*...

2000 A.D.
Credit Card:
SCRIPT ROBOT
PAT MILLS
ART ROBOT
RON SMITH
LETTERING ROBOT
TOM FRAME
COMPU·73E

JUDGE DREDD
IN MONKEY BUSINESS AT THE
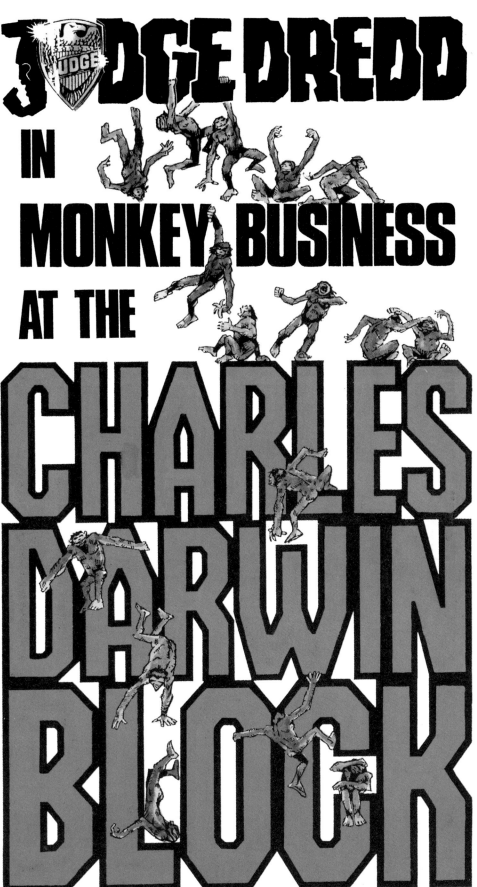

CHARLES DARWIN BLOCK

THE CHARLES DARWIN BLOCK HAS GONE APE!

PROFESSOR E. NORTHCOTE FRIBB LIVED IN APARTMENT 66C, CHARLES DARWIN BLOCK. IT WAS EARLIER THAT DAY HE HAD MADE HIS **MOMENTOUS DISCOVERY** —

I'VE DONE IT! I'VE ISOLATED AN **ENZYME** WHICH CAN **REVERSE** THE PROCESS OF **EVOLUTION**!

WITH IT I WILL AT LAST BE ABLE TO UNRAVEL THE MYSTERY OF **MAN'S ORIGINS**! WERE OUR ANCESTORS **APES** — OR **FISH**?

HMMM, UNUSUAL SMELL... RATHER LIKE SPAGHETTI SAUCE...

FOR PROFESSOR FRIBB, IT WAS ONE SMELL TOO MANY —

I-I'M GOING **HAIRY**!

SMASH!

WITH EACH PASSING SECOND, **THOUSANDS OF YEARS** OF EVOLUTIONARY CHANGE WERE **DROPPING AWAY**!

THE **FRIBB ENZYME** (AS IT CAME TO BE CALLED) WAS A TRUE MIRACLE OF 22ND CENTURY SCIENCE —

THE GREATEST BREAKTHROUGH SINCE INFLATABLE KNEECAPS!

SADLY, PROFESSOR E. NORTHCOTE FRIBB NO LONGER CARED —

UHHHHHH!

THE POWERFUL ENZYME WAS SUCKED INTO THE BLOCK VENTILATION DUCTS —

WHERE LEROY MCDONALD OF THE **SWEETAIR VENTILATION CO.** WAS CARRYING OUT ROUTINE MAINTENANCE...

MM-MMM! SOMEBODY'S COOKIN' SPAGHETTI DOWN THERE!

UHHH !

IT WAS DURING LEROY MCDONALD'S EXUBERANT DISPLAY OF THE PRIMITIVE ART OF **SWINGING** THAT THE **AIR OUTLET** CAME INTO CLOSE CONTACT WITH THE **AIR INLET** —

AND CIRCULATED THE **FRIBB ENZYME** THROUGHOUT THE BUILDING —

ALL RIGHT! WHICH OF YOU CHILDREN HAS BROUGHT SPAGHETTI INTO THIS CLASSROOM? IF I'VE TOLD YOU ONCE, I'VE... TOLD YOU...

UHHHH !

EEP !

EEEP !

ALL OVER THE CHARLES DARWIN BLOCK, PRIMITIVE INSTINCTS TOOK OVER —

WHAT'S GOING ON? TENANTS WILL RETURN TO THEIR APARTMENTS IMMEDIATELY!

MR AND MRS ANDREWS! YOU MUST NOT KNOCK HOLES IN YOUR WALL!

REALLY, MR ANDREWS! THROWING CARETAKER DROIDS OUT OF WINDOWS IS A REPORTABLE OFFENCE!

AN HOUR LATER, JUDGES HAD CORDONED OFF THE WHOLE BLOCK —

AS FAR AS WE CAN MAKE OUT THE WHOLE BLOCK IS AFFECTED, DREDD. WE TRIED SENDING JUDGES IN —

UHH!

UHH!

UHH!

THAT'S THEM ON THE FOURTH FLOOR!

CHANCES ARE THE CONTAMINATION IS AIR-SPREAD! **RESPIRATOR DOWN!**

IF I'M RIGHT, YOU'LL HEAR FROM ME!

IN APARTMENT 7AK, UNEMPLOYED EXECUTIVE THEODORE WAINWRIGHT HAD DISCOVERED HIS ANTIQUE HUNTING GUN —

IN THE DIM RECESSES OF HIS MIND, THEODORE KNEW THIS STRANGE CONTRAPTION HAD SOME PURPOSE...

THEODORE'S DISCOVERY GOES NO FURTHER. BUT NEXT DOOR IN 7AL, UNEMPLOYED SYNTHETIC FOOD TASTER BOB KEMPINSKI HAD MADE ANOTHER IMPORTANT DISCOVERY —

FIRE!

ALWAYS QUICK ON THE UPTAKE, BOB LOST NO TIME EXPERIMENTING WITH HIS DANGEROUS DISCOVERY —

UHH! UHHH!

RESPIRATOR WORKING SO FAR! GOING TO NEED FIVE HUNDRED MEN TO CLEAN UP THIS MESS —

GOING TO NEED SOME ZOO KEEPERS TOO!

TRY THE NEXT LEVEL. GOT TO FIND THE SOURCE OF THE CONTAMINATION!

GARAGE

BY THE TIME DREDD REACHED LEVEL TWO, BOB KEMPINSKI HAD BLAZED A PATH TO THE GROUND FLOOR GARAGE —

HERE, YOU! PUT THAT OUT!

UHH!

IN THE STRUGGLE, BOB'S BRAND WENT FLYING —

NO, THAT PETROL TANK...

UHH?

WHOOMPH

BOB KEMPINSKI HAD LEARNED THE DANGER OF PLAYING WITH FIRE.

NEXT PROG: THE ORIGIN OF SPECIES!

35

JUDGE DREDD

IN MONKEY BUSINESS AT THE **CHARLES DARWIN BLOCK**

EVOLUTION HAS TURNED *BACKWARDS* AT THE *CHARLES DARWIN BLOCK*, AND THE OCCUPANTS HAVE REVERTED TO THE *APE* STATE. DREDD GOES TO INVESTIGATE, WHEN —

WHOOMPH!

EXPLOSION IN THE GROUND FLOOR GARAGE! THAT'S WHERE DREDD IS!

2000 A.D.
Credit Card:

SCRIPT ROBOT
T. B. GROVER

ART ROBOT
MIKE McMAHON

LETTERING ROBOT
TOM FRAME

COMPU·73E

STILL ALIVE — JUST! BUT IF WE DON'T ACT FAST, THESE APES ARE GOING TO *TOTAL* THE WHOLE BLOCK!

DREDD HERE! RESPIRATOR IS WORKING AGAINST THE CONTAMINATION!

GET FIRE TEAMS IN HERE, AND MORE JUDGES!

LOTS MORE JUDGES!

NNNH!

As the fire teams moved in, unemployed plasteen worker Judith Dobble in apartment 6R had a clever idea —

AAAGH!

LOOK OUT! THEY'RE THROWING STUFF!

Judith was well-known for her sharp sense of humour. Some vestige of it still remained in her now-bestial brain —

UHH! UHH! UHHHH!

Upstairs in 7R, the Bolsover family eagerly followed Judith's lead —

UHH!

UHHH!

All except Granny Bolsover, who had accidentally stuck her head through the vidset —

On the 4th floor, Judges Nestor, Martin and Garsonovitz, who had inadvertently entered without respirators, played it cool —

THEY'RE ALL AT IT! WE'LL BE CRUSHED TO DEATH!

TRAIN YOUR FIRE HOSES ON THEM! NO SHOOTING UNLESS YOU HAVE TO!

STOMM! WHAT HAPPENED HERE, DREDD?

THEY HAD TO BE SUBDUED — FOR THEIR OWN PROTECTION! GET TO WORK, MEN! I WANT THIS BLOCK BROUGHT UNDER CONTROL!

DREDD'S HELMET COM CRACKLED TO LIFE —

ATTENTION, JUDGE DREDD! THE BLOCK REGISTER SHOWS A PROFESSOR E. NORTHCOTE FRIBB IN 66C! RUMOUR IS HE WAS WORKING ON AN ENZYME WHICH WOULD TURN EVOLUTION BACKWARDS!

THAT COULD BE THE SOURCE OF THE CONTAMINATION! I'LL CHECK IT OUT!

RAMP TO ALL LEVELS

ON LEVEL 29, UNEMPLOYED "OLIVE OIL IMPORTER" COSMO CORLEONE HAD BARRICADED THE STAIRS AND WAS CHARGING A TOLL FOR SAFE PASSAGE —

UHH! UHHH!

CREEP WANTS A BANANA —

PAID WITH THANKS!

AS DREDD NEARED THE 66TH FLOOR —

CONTAMINATION'S GETTING STRONGER! THEY'RE REGRESSING TO THE LOWER ANIMAL STAGES!

IN 66A, UNEMPLOYED ACROBATIC TROUPE *THE FLYING HENDERSONS* HEARD DREDD'S APPROACH —

A HAPPY FAMILY, EARLIER THAT DAY THEY HAD BEEN PREPARING FOR A PLEASANT PICNIC IN CHARLES DARWIN BLOCK PARK—

THINGS HAD RADICALLY CHANGED FOR THE FLYING HENDERSONS —

NOW ALL THEY CRAVED WAS FLESH!

SEVERE REGRESSION!

THERE'S NO SAVING THESE POOR DEVILS!

MORE OF THEM — AND WORSE! HATE TO THINK WHAT I'LL FIND IN 66C!

DROKK!

40

ON THE WORKBENCH, PROFESSOR E. NORTHCOTE FRIBB'S APPARATUS BUBBLED ON, DRIPPING OUT THE ENZYME WHICH HAD TURNED CHARLES DARWIN BLOCK INTO A NAKED JUNGLE.

ON THE FLOOR LAY PROFESSOR FRIBB. HIS SEARCH FOR THE ORIGIN OF SPECIES HAD BEEN A COMPLETE SUCCESS!

SOME KIND OF... GIANT AMOEBA!

DREDD HERE! I WANT THIS BUILDING EVACUATED — REPEAT — EVACUATED!

KKRASH!

WITHIN AN HOUR, THE LAST RECOGNISABLY HUMAN OCCUPANTS WERE BEING HERDED FROM THE CHARLES DARWIN BLOCK —

CALL THE FIRE FIGHTERS OFF! LET IT BURN!

I KNOW THE FRIBB ENZYME WAS DANGEROUS — BUT BURNING THE WHOLE BLOCK, DREDD...?

YOU SAW WHAT IT DID. BETTER SAFE THAN SORRY!

RE-EVOLVING THE SURVIVORS OF CHARLES DARWIN BLOCK WAS A MATTER THAT WOULD OCCUPY MEGA-CITY SCIENTISTS FOR A LONG TIME TO COME.

MEANWHILE, THERE REMAINED ONLY ONE THING TO DO —

BOOK HIM!

JUDGE DREDD

THE WEATHER MAN

PART 1

SINCE THE DESTRUCTION OF MEGA-CITY ONE'S WEATHER CONTROL, WEATHER FORECASTING HAD BECOME RATHER A HAPHAZARD SCIENCE —

AS USUAL, VIDDERS, IN ALL SECTORS WHERE WEATHER CONTROL HAS BEEN RE-ESTABLISHED, WE CAN EXPECT A FINE DRY DAY, WITH DAYTIME TEMPERATURES VARYING BETWEEN 20·1 AND 20·15 DEGREES.

ELSEWHERE, YOUR GUESS IS AS GOOD AS MINE!

WHAT WE CAN TELL YOU IS — AVOID SECTOR 61! THAT NASTY SNOW BLIZZARD IS STILL THERE.

AND THERE'S A VAST RADIOACTIVE CLOUD SWEEPING UP FROM THE DEAD SOUTH. YOU SOUTHSIDERS REMEMBER THOSE NOSE FILTERS AND ANTI-RAD PILLS!

APART FROM THAT, EXPECT THE UNEXPECTED — AND LET'S KEEP THAT DEATH TOLL DOWN, HUH, FOLKS?

SCRIPT
T B GROVER
ART
RON SMITH
LETTERING
T FRAME

IN THE ABSENCE OF WEATHER CONTROL'S REFINED TECHNIQUES, ATMOSPHERIC DISTORTIONS WROUGHT BY THE APOCALYPSE WAR CAN CAUSE SUDDEN FREAK CHANGES IN WEATHER —

DREDD TO CONTROL! SPOT OF BAD WEATHER SPRINGING UP VICINITY FROTH STREET!

DREDD MAKES HIS ARREST —

CONTROL! WHEN IN GRUD'S NAME ARE WE GOING TO GET THIS WEATHER FIXED?

BUT THERE ARE SOME WHO ENJOY THE FREAK CONDITIONS — EVEN EXULT IN THEM!

THUNDER ROAR! LIGHTNING CRACK!

FANTASTICO!

VUNDERBAR!

ONE SUCH MAN IS CARL HEINZ PILCHARDS-IN-TOMATO-SAUCE CLAYDERMAN —

AHHH! THE MAGNIFICENT VUNDERS OF NATURE! HOW THEY FIRE MY IMAGINATION — GIF TO ME MY GREATEST EFFER INSPIRATION!

THE LINE BETWEEN GENIUS AND MADNESS IS A FINE ONE. CLAYDERMAN HAS CROSSED IT — AND THEN SOME!

CARL HEINZ PILCHARDS-IN-TOMATO-SAUCE CLAYDERMAN'S VEATHER SYMPHONY! MY MASTER VORK! THE GREATEST SPECTACLE THE WORLD HAS EFFER VITNESSED!

TONIGHT, IT VILL GET ITS FIRST PERFORMANCE!

IT VILL ALSO BE ITS LAST PERFORMANCE, OF COURSE!

BUT HIMMEL! VOT A PERFORMANCE!

THE CONCERT APPLICATION HAD BEEN PROCESSED THROUGH JUSTICE DEPARTMENT'S CENSORS WITHOUT SUSPICION —

I SEE "PITS" CLAYDERMAN HAS COMPOSED ANOTHER SYMPHONY.

HOPE IT'S BETTER THAN HIS LAST. TWELVE ROBOTIC CHICKENS LOCKED INSIDE A PIANO...

APPROVED

NOT APPROVED

YEAH – EASY LISTENING IT WASN'T!

CONCERT APPLICATION

WORK

CLAYDERMAN'S SYMPHONY

APPROVED

ON THE EVENING OF THE CONCERT, TWO JUDGES WERE ROUTINELY ASSIGNED TO AUDIENCE CONTROL –

STUMM GAS – RIOT FOAM – DAY STICK. RIGHT. I'M READY!

RECKON WE'LL NEED ALL THIS GEAR WITH THESE CULTURE BUGS?

CLAYDERMAN'S WEATHER SYMPHONY

††† TONITE ONLY! † † †

TAKE IT FROM ME, DENNY – THE BUGS ARE OFTEN THE WORST!

GWYN

IF THE JUDGES HAD HAD ONLY A GLIMMER OF WHAT WAS TO COME, THEY WOULD HAVE CANCELLED THE CONCERT FORTHWITH!

CITIZENS – I GIVE YOU THE MAESTRO HIMSELF – CARL HEINZ PILCHARDS-IN-TOMATO-SAUCE CLAYDERMAN!

THANK YOU AND GOOT EVENING! TONIGHT, I VELCOME YOU TO VITNESS – NO! TO PARTICIPATE IN – THE GREATEST ARTISTIC ACHIEVEMENT OF ALL TIME!

VEN I TALK ABOUT ART, I DO NOT MEAN THE USUAL HOOHA VICH VE VAIN HUMANS TALK ABOUT!

NO! I MEAN REAL ART! NATURE'S ART! THE MAGNIFICENT CRACK OF THE THUNDERBOLT! THE SEARING, DEADLY BEAUTY OF THE LIGHTNING FLASH!

VY, THERE IS MORE ART IN VUN SNOWFLAKE THAN IN ALL THE VORKS OF VILLY DUM-DUM SHAKESPEARE!

GET ON WITH IT, PILCHARD! I PAID GOOD CREDS TO LISTEN TO THIS!

WHAACK!

WEED OUT THE TROUBLEMAKERS AT ONCE – THAT'S THE ONLY POLICY!

47

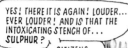

54

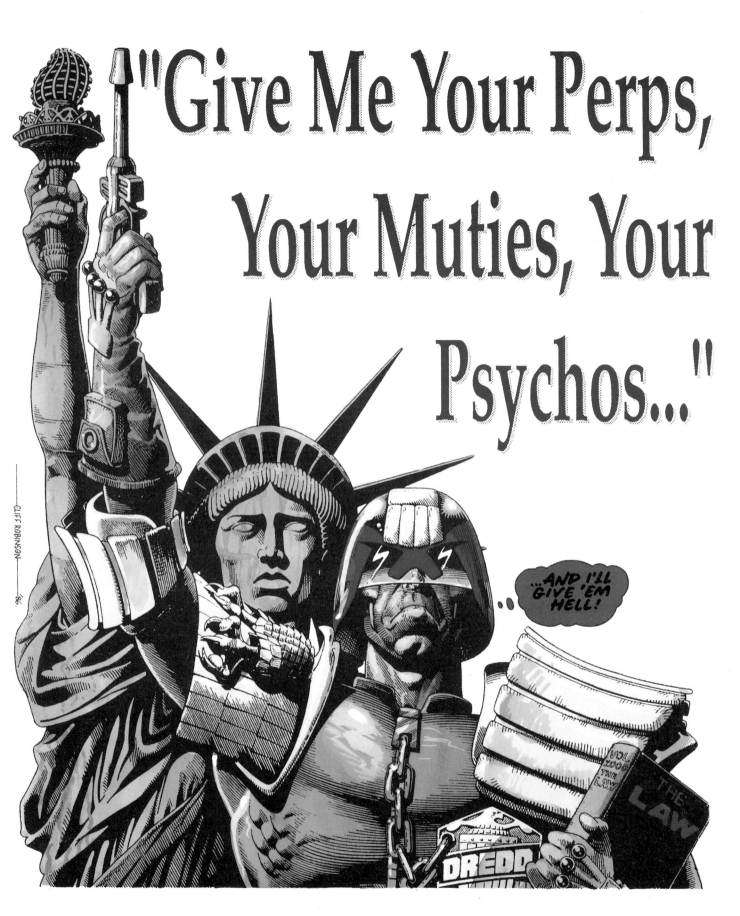

MEGA-CITY ONE. AUGUST 2102 A.D.
TEMPERATURES WERE HIGH – BUT TEMPERS IN THE THATCHIT FAMILY WERE EVEN HIGHER –

GROOGH! DAMMIT, WOMAN – I CAN'T DRINK **HOT** SYNTHI-CAFF ON A DAY LIKE THIS!

WAUUGH!

MUM, DOESN'T ELEANOR LOOK SILLY WITH MY SOYA PORRIDGE ON HER HEAD?

YOU LITTLE **VILLAIN!** I'LL PASTE YOUR EAR!

DAMMIT, IS NOBODY LISTENING TO ME?

HEY, YOU CITIZENS! STOP THAT SQUABBLING!

THIS IS YOUR HOME COMPUTER AGGRO UNIT REPORTING A THATCHIT **AGGRESSION LEVEL** OF AN UNHEALTHY 14%.... ADVICE: YOUR LOCAL **AGGRO DOME** OPENS TODAY. TRY IT.

THE AGGRO DOME – LATEST IN A LONG LINE OF COMMERCIAL ATTEMPTS TO CASH IN ON – AND CONTROL – THE SEETHING PASSIONS BRED IN A CITY OF OVER **800 MILLION** CLOSE-PACKED PEOPLE!

AGGRO DOME

2000 A.D.
Credit Card:
SCRIPT ROBOT ALVIN GAUNT
ART ROBOT MIKE McMAHON
LETTERING ROBOT TOM FRAME
COMPU-73E

INSIDE, THEIR PE... VIOLENC... FOR A F...

CHOP WOOD

COP THIS, MISS PERKINS!

VAPE A TEACHER

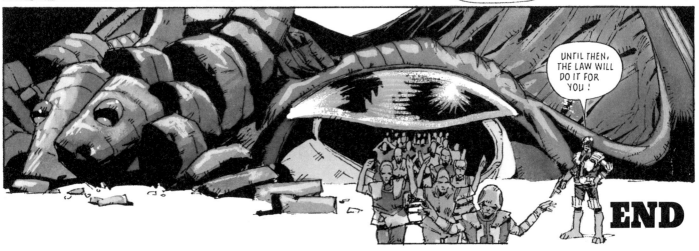

DEP.LEG. B-38.073-90